Mini Minds Dinosaur Illustrations by
Rachael Sligo

Kindasaurus saves Christmas

Kindasaurus saves Christmas

A Mini Minds Matter Book

MINI MINDS *Matter*

THE CALM MIND CONSULTANT

by
Julie Robinson & Mandy Worsley
Designed by Celia J-Hale

Produced by
Johnston-Hale Publications
in the United Kingdom

www.johnston-hale.co.uk
Design by Johnston-Hale Publications

Issue 2
First Published in 2021

Cover Design by Celia J-Hale
Dinosaurs designed by Rachael Sligo for Mini Minds Matter UK Ltd.
Authors Mandy Worsley and Julie Robinson

This book is part of a series of mindfulness books aimed
to assist educational and childcare settings in supporting
the mental health of pre-schoolers and young children.

Johnston Hale
PUBLICATIONS

www.minimindsmatter.org.uk

Preface

This book has been written by the Mini Minds Matter team, to accompany the Mini Minds Matter methods that are part of the programme that we offer. It can be read by children individually or as part of a group activity in an educational setting.

At the end of this book you will find resources that may be useful to you and ways that you can join the Mini Minds Matter membership to support the mental health of your little ones.

Acknowledgements

We would like to thank our beloved Mini Minds partners for supporting us in our journey of helping little minds prosper worldwide, one establishment at a time.

Together, you are part of a movement to protect the emotional health of the next generation and make the world a better and happier place for us all.

Kindasaurus saves Christmas

Julie Robinson

Mandy Worsley

Can you find me and my friends in the story?

Hello!
Let me tell you my name.

I am Kindasaurus.

Would you like to play a game?

To help me share kindness at Christmas.

Some cheeky elves have hidden it away!

We need to look high.

We need to look low.

On a kindness treasure
hunt we must go!

So open your eyes and follow the clues.

All different colours!

Reds, greens and blues.

Can you see it anywhere?

Let us look for the first clue here.

Hip hip hurray, you found the first clue!
Now you know what to do!

Pop it in Santa's sack.
It will still be there when we come back!

And off we go, for clue number 2!

What colour is the next surprise?

Look very carefully with your eyes...

Well done!

You have found clue number 2!

Kindasaurus is so happy for you!

So let's set off again for the hunt to find the third clue.

Where oh where could it be?

Maybe it is behind the big Christmas tree?

Well done you found it!

Hop, skip and jump to number 4!

Is it behind that big red door?

Let us see what you have found so far.

That spells kind.
Only 4 more letters still to find!

Let us move around the tree,
what can you see?

Can you solve clue five's mystery?

Peeping out from behind that flower!
Finding clues is your super power!

Three more left to find!
So let us hurry, don't get left behind!

I spy with my little eye...
clue number 6 way up high,
shining like the moon in the sky!

Where oh where is clue number 7?
Look down from heaven,
to the ground...

Where Mr. Snowman can be found!
Look at his buttons- could that be one?

Yes it is! Oh what fun!

Now on to clue number 8.
This treasure hunt, sure is great!

But remember to look out for the cheeky elf...
Who came down from his shelf...

So let us hurry and find the last clue.
I am sure by now, you know what to do!

Now... What can you see, up ahead?
Could that be... Santa's sled?!

Great job finding clue number 8!
Kindasaurus says "You're doing great!"

Don't stop now, put it in the sack.
You now have 8 clues, so let's head back.

Kindasaurus thinks you're super and wants your
help again next year!

Even the elves are giving you a cheer!

Hip hip hurray, you have found the best gift of all...

Kindness

To many, it may only seem small.
But if you are kind in many different ways,
it will feel like Christmas every day.

Remember, kindness is not just for Christmas Day,
but something for us all, each day of the year.
So thank you for your gift of kindness and
spreading the Christmas Cheer.

The End

Kindasaurus Saves Christmas

Hello I'm here to save Xmas
I think I may need your help.
Do you think you can be gracious?
And collect the magic without a Yelp

Christmas is a special time
I know you feel the same
So let's plan a journey at bedtime
To help keep the Christmas name

I'm Kindasaurus the dinosaur
I'm kind as kind can be
Will you help to collect Christmas cheer
before unkindness makes Christmas flee?

We need you to believe in Christmas
The fun, gifts , joy and the trees
Kindness deeds are our business
So being kind seems to hold the key.

How many kind deeds can you do
To lift some Christmas cheer
I bet you can do more than two
At least ten without any fear!

Oh wow you have been amazing
Spreading all of your kind deeds
The spirit of Christmas is worth saving
kindness and love have planted the seeds

Santa now has a sparkle
And a twinkle in his eye
You have helped to save Christmas
So it's time to say good bye.

Fun Time

Can you spot the differences?

There are 5

Merry

Learn to draw this tree on your own piece of paper

Step 1

Step 2

Step 3

Step 4

Step 5

Learn to draw this tree on your own piece of paper

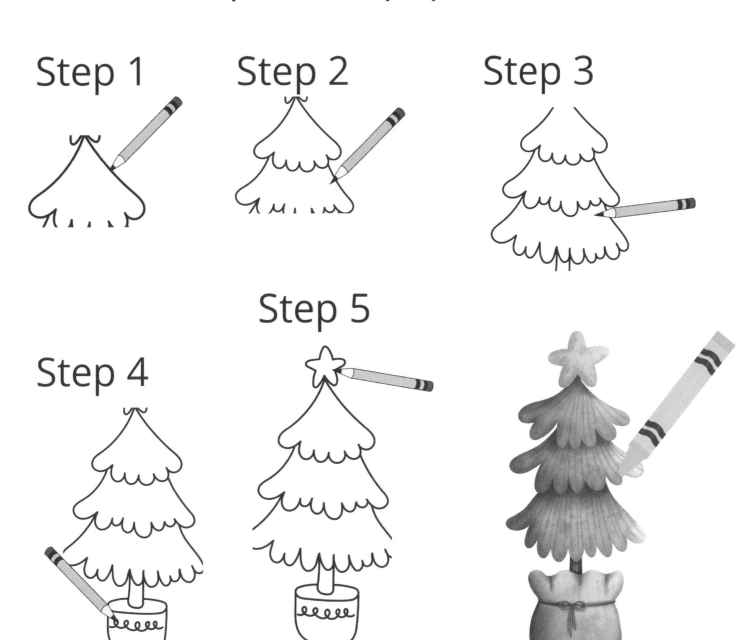

Step 1

Step 2

Step 3

Step 4

Step 5

Norwegian Christmas Hearts

You will need scissors and some glue and an adult too!

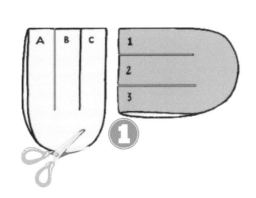

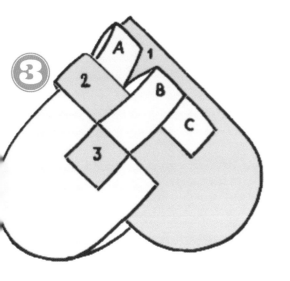

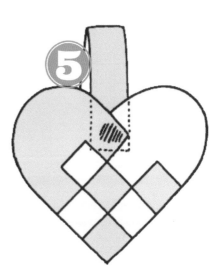

Traditional Gingerbread Recipe

Make cookies or try building your
own house?

Celia's Viking Gingerbread

150 g unsalted butter, softened
150 g caster sugar
70 ml treacle
50 ml golden syrup
75 ml whole milk
1 medium egg yolk
450 g plain flour
2 tsp ground ginger
2 tsp cinnamon
1 tsp cardamom, ground to a fine powder
1 tsp bicarbonate of soda
1 tsp ground cloves
¼ tsp finely ground black pepper
½ tsp fine sea salt

Celia's Viking Gingerbread

- Melt it all in a pot first.
- Then add in the dry ingredients and stir well (the mixture will be sticky!)
- Then wrap up the dough in cling film and put it in the fridge overnight or 3 hours to chill
- Once the dough is chilled, heat your oven to 165C.
- Roll out the dough onto a baking sheet really thin as you are aiming for thin and crispy cookies.
- cut out into your chosen shape or use google for a stencil for a gingerbread house!
- Bake the cookies on the top shelf for about 10 minutes. If it is not crispy enough, leave it in the oven for a couple more minutes. You will need about 3 -4 baking trays depending on the size of your cookie cutters.
- Take your gingerbread biscuits out of the oven and cool them on a wire rack.
- These will keep for about 4 weeks in an airtight container.
- Post your results on social media with **#minivikings**

The End

MINI MINDS

Matter

Become a Mini Minds Matter Partner today:

https://www.minimindsmatter.org.uk/

Mini Minds Oliiki Partnership

The first 1000 days, from conception to two are life-changing days! So much learning and development happens during this time.

Baby's brains are being formed and they are starting out on a journey of discovery and learning adventures. And they need to learn everything; from the earliest days in the womb, they are listening to sounds and feel the movement of their mother as she goes about her daily life.

They are feeling the environment that their parents are providing for them.

Once born, parents and carers continue to set the context and environment for learning for the child. Calm, happy, nurturing environments (such as those created through Mini Minds) enable children to feel safe and secure and this allows them to open their brains ready to receive the learning opportunities that present themselves on a daily basis.

Once the context is set, giving the child playful learning adventures allows them to develop the skills, knowledge and understanding to grow and develop to the full.

When parents and caregivers understand the learning a child is gaining from each tiny playful moment they are able to support them to gain the most from the interaction so helping them build skill on skill.

The Oliiki app is an app for parents, parents-to-be and carers to spark their babies' adventures in learning and build their parenting confidence one play activity at a time.

It ensures strong foundations of learning grounded in science and delivered through play so that children can reach their full potential and fly.

Clare Stead
Founder and Creator of the Oliiki app

www.oliikiapp.com

Useful Links

Mini Minds Matter
www.minimindsmatter.org.uk

Build your baby's brain in the first 1000 days of life
www.oliikiapp.com

Nicky Kay
Holistic Wellness Advocate
www.nickykay.co.uk

Emma Stott
Wellbeing and Parenting Coach
www.facebook.com/wellbeingandparenting

Johnston-Hale

PUBLICATIONS

Submit your manuscript to johnston.hale@gmail.com
or visit www.johnston-hale.co.uk

Printed in Great Britain
by Amazon

11330110R00049